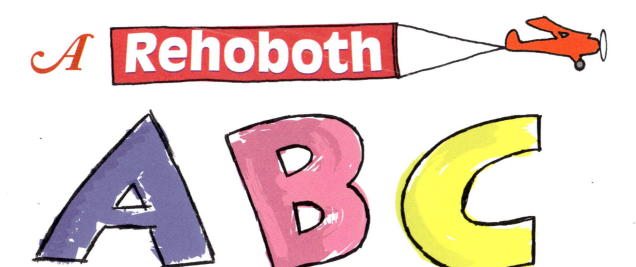

A Rehoboth ABC

by Nancy Sakaduski

Illustrations by Emory Au

Copyright ©2013 by Nancy Sakaduski
Illustrations copyright ©2013 by Emory Au
All rights reserved.

ISBN-10: 0615786820
ISBN-13: 978-0615786827

Printed in the United States of America
Cat & Mouse Press
Lewes, Delaware
www.catandmousepress.com

A Playful Publisher

*Having fun in Rehoboth
is as easy as A-B-C!*

A is for arcade

Frog flipper, mole whacker, ball roller, prize!
Wheels spinning, tickets winning, quarters on the fly!

Snow cones, crab homes, tee shirts and towels
Waves crashing, strollers dashing, "I want candy" howls.

C is for custard

Chocolate dipping, cone dripping, sidewalk slipping fun
Icy, creamy, silky, dreamy, yum, yum, yum!

D is for dolphins

Fins flapping, tails slapping, noses popping—where?
Water slopping, bodies flopping—now they're over there!

E is for explore

Sand sifts, shovel lifts, pour in the pail
Down we go, water shows, better start to bail.

F is for fireworks

Rockets roar, missiles soar, and then the colors bloom
Sky screamer, night squealer, Fourth of July kaboom!

G is for gull

Wind catching, feather scratching,
French fry snatching swoop
Floating, flying, gliding, diving, watch out for the ...

 is for **hermit crab**

Pale shell, snail shell, washed up in the tide
Who's to know what doesn't show—a tiny crab inside.

I is for in

I'm not ready, please don't make me, I am scared, you know
There's my Dad, it's not so bad. Ready, set, let's go!

J is for jellyfish

Jiggly jelly, wiggly belly, squishy squashy blob
Look—don't touch—its sting hurts much,
this spongy gooey glob.

K is for kite

Twirling, curling, diving, gliding, soaring through the air
Swooping, swaying, not obeying, that is so unfair.

L is for lotion

Creams and squirts, sprays and spurts, sun up in the skies
Lather, slather, doesn't matter. Just not in my eyes!

M is for mini-golf

Club swinging, ball zinging, this is lots of fun
Turns and bumps and hills and humps and then
a hole-in-one!

N is for **nap**

No, no, no! Want to swim, want to play, want to go, go, go
No time for sleep, no time to doze,
want to put back on my clothes.

O is for **ocean**

Frothing, foaming, rushing, roaming, tickling at your toes
Silly tide, it can't decide. In it comes and out it goes.

P is for **pack**

Pails and paddles, bags and boards, pile them way up high
Snacks and hats, towels and mats stacked nearly to the sky.

Q is for quench

Water, water, everywhere but nothing I can drink
I want soda, juice, or milk, or water from the sink.

R is for rides

Horses up, horses down, helicopters, swings
Cars and trucks and boats that float and bells that ring-a-ding.

S is for **sandcastle**

Sand mound, pack down, towers high and turrets round
Bucket, truck it, banner stuck it, high up on the crown.

T is for taffy

Banana, chocolate, orange, grape, watermelon too
Peanut butter—have another. Which one is for you?

 is for **umbrella**

Up it goes but then it blows, goes rolling out of reach
Twisting, twirling, spinning, swirling, whirling down the beach.

V is for vest

Bright vest, light vest, do I have to wear it vest
Yes you do, it is brand new, let's put it to the test.

W is for waves

Here it comes, let's all run, it's coming with a crash
Wade out, watch out, jump out! Now it's time for us to dash!

X marks the spot

Treasure left by buccaneers, buried under sand for years
Will you find gold coins or bars? Maybe, matey. Aarrrrrr!

Y is for yogurt

Cookie crumbles, candy jumbles, brownies, nuts, and stars
Sours, gummies, chips, and yummies—
don't spill in the car!

Z is for zzzzzz

Umbrella's closed up, castle's washed up, tummy's full up, time to go up. Night night.

Nancy Day Sakaduski | *Author*

Nancy writes for children and adults and has authored 17 published books. One of her children's books, *Passport to History: Ancient Greece,* was named best social studies book by the Society of School Librarians International and "Mapping the Mind," which appeared in *Odyssey* Magazine, won the Society of Children's Book Writers and Illustrators Award for Nonfiction. She is a member of the Rehoboth Beach Writers' Guild and lives in Lewes, Delaware.

Emory Au | *Illustrator*

Emory is a Columbus College of Art & Design graduate. He is an award-winning graphic designer as well as an accomplished fine artist. Emory designed this book and also created the Cat & Mouse Press logo. He lives in Hockessin, Delaware.

Cat & Mouse Press | *Publisher*

Cat & Mouse Press is a small publishing company based in Lewes, Delaware. Our goal is to create fun, humorous, entertaining, and engaging books and other materials for adults and children. We focus on titles of interest to residents and visitors of the Delaware Cape region.

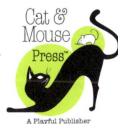

Made in the USA
Charleston, SC
27 April 2013